Put it Back, Jack!

Written and illustrated by

Roey Ebert

To Jack
May your world be always filled with perfect surprises.
And, to GMVLP, with love and thanks for being perfectly full of surprises.
My illustrations are dedicated to Duke, my amazing animal expert.

Put it Back, Jack
Copyright © 2012 Rosemary R. Ebert
Print ISBN: 978-1-61633-217-4; 1616332174
eBook ISBN: 978-1-61633-218-1; 1616332182
January 2012
Published in the United States of America

GUARDIAN ANGEL PUBLISHING, INC.
12430 Tesson Ferry Road #186
Saint Louis, Missouri 63128 USA
http://www.GuardianAngelPublishing.com

Jack and Max took a walk into the woods.
Max held Jack's hand.
Max showed Jack the raccoon tracks on the path.
Jack stepped on them.
Max showed Jack the tiny blue lizard. Jack picked it up.
Max showed Jack the hawk flying in the sky.
Jack jumped up to catch him. He couldn't.

Max took Jack near the tiny stream.
He told Jack to be very quiet.
A baby deer was drinking water. Jack smiled.
He loved the baby deer. He wanted to take it home.
Max told Jack that was silly. Deer live in the woods.
But Jack did not listen to Max.

Jack went over to the baby deer.
It was so small—small enough for Jack to pick up.
Max told Jack it was time to go.
Jack looked at the baby deer and waved goodbye.
Jack would miss him.

Max heard an owl and went to look.
Jack picked up the baby deer and put it in his coat pocket.
Jack giggled.
Max told Jack they should leave now. It would be dark soon.

Max could not hold on to Jack's hand.
Jack was too squirmy.
They walked on the path through the woods.
The sky was dark when they got home.

Jack asked for a drink.
Jack's mom gave him a drink in a cup.
Max saw Jack pour the drink into a bottle.
Jack asked for a snack—a big snack.
Jack's mom gave him some carrots.
Max watched Jack put the carrots in his pocket.

Jack asked for a ball to play with.
Mom gave him the soccer ball.
Max wondered who Jack was going to play with.
Max watched Jack go down to the basement.
Jack closed the door softly behind him.

Max followed quietly. He sneaked down the basement stairs.
Jack!
Jack was feeding the baby deer a bottle.

Max told Jack they had to put it back.
Deer live in the woods.
Jack fed the baby deer a carrot.
The baby deer kissed Jack. Jack giggled.

**Max kicked the soccer ball.
The deer kicked it back. Max laughed.
Jack, Max, and baby deer played soccer in the basement.
Jack and Max's mom called that it was time for bed.**

Jack and Max asked if they could sleep downstairs.
Max put a blanket around Jack and the deer.
Jack hugged the baby deer all night.

When the sun came through the windows, Max woke Jack up.
The baby deer was still sleeping.
Jack picked it up and put the deer in his coat.
Max held Jack's hand. They followed the path into the woods.

Jack saw the raccoon tracks.
Jack saw the lizard.
Jack saw the hawk and the owl.
Jack saw a mommy deer!
Max helped Jack place baby deer on the path.
Baby deer ran to his mommy.

Jack waved goodbye.
Baby deer ran back to Max
and kicked an acorn.
Max kicked it to Jack.
Jack kicked it to baby deer.
They all smiled.

CPSIA information can be obtained
at www.ICGtesting.com
Printed in the USA
LVIC04n2339100517
534083LV00001B/3